D1481799

QUEST FOR TREASURE IN THE CAYMAN ISLANDS

Adventures of Riley

Photographs by
Amanda Lumry

Story by
Laura Hurwitz
& Amanda Lumry

Illustrations by
Sarah McIntyre

EaglemonT
Press

In memory of
Hope Glidden-Borden MBE (Miss Hope)
and to the children of Cayman

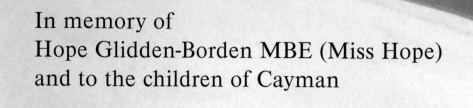

© 2002 by Eaglemont Press
Photographs by Amanda Lumry
Illustrations by Sarah McIntyre

First edition published 2002 by Eaglemont Press.
PMB 741
15600 NE 8th #B-1
Bellevue, WA 98008
(425) 462-6618

ISBN 0-9662257-5-9
Library of Congress Control Number: 2002110855

info@eaglemontpress.com
www.eaglemontpress.com
www.adventuresofriley.com

Editing and layout by Emily McGalliard
Printed and bound in Hong Kong by C&C Offset
Printing Co., Ltd.

"Hello, Riley!" his mother greeted him. "How was your day?"

"Okay," he sighed as he gathered the mail. "The playground was too icy. Do you think it will ever warm up?"

A blue envelope with Riley's name on it caught his attention. "Mom! Uncle Max invited me on a trip to the Cayman Islands!"

Hello, Carrot Top!
How would you like to join us in the Cayman Islands during winter break? See you there!
Your crazy uncle,
Max

"That is fantastic! Can you bring me back a Cayman Islands rum cake? I hear they are world famous."

"It is so hot here!" said Riley.

"Let's change into our swimsuits really fast! Mum, can we go swimming right away?" Alice asked.

"Sure, dear," Aunt Martha smiled.

Minutes later, everyone plunged into the clear blue water. "Uncle Max, why is our hotel called the Cayman Treasure Resort?" asked Riley.

"Hundreds of years ago, pirates stopped here to hide their plunder and feast on turtles," Uncle Max replied.

"Oh, those poor turtles!" Alice said.

Riley wasn't thinking about the turtles. "Plunder? Do you mean treasure? Do you think there is still some here?" he asked.

"Keep a sharp lookout. You never know," said Uncle Max.

That evening they drove to a
restaurant that was perched over
a lagoon. Just inside the door, a
colorful parrot greeted them.

"Hello," said Alice.
"Hello," the parrot
echoed back.
"Wow," said Riley.
"That is one smart bird!"

The next day, they decided to learn more about turtles at the Turtle Farm. A guide showed them several tanks with different sized turtles. Some were tiny enough to hold in their hands, and others were big enough to ride.

"Turtles have always been important to the people of Cayman," the guide told the visitors. "The peg-legged pirate turtle is the islands' symbol." Riley's eyes widened at the mention of pirates.

The green sea turtle gets its name from the color of its fat.

The sex of green sea turtles is determined by water temperature. Warmer temperatures produce females; cooler temperatures produce males.

Green sea turtles can weigh up to 700 pounds, or 320 kilograms.

In George Town, Cayman's capital city, the group wandered through many shops.

"Oh, I love this turtle T-shirt!" cried Alice.

"Don't I look like a pirate in this bandanna?" asked Riley.

"Speaking of pirates," smiled Uncle Max, "maybe we will find some treasure if we take a look underwater."

everything around, just as if you were to fill a glass of water with sand and shells and shake it up."

"Welcome aboard the Atlantis submarine," said the guide. "We are going one hundred feet below the surface today. You will see many colorful fish, sponges and coral."

"What is that cool-looking fish?" asked Alice.

"It's a queen angelfish," answered the guide.

"Are we going to see any pirate shipwrecks?" asked Riley.

The guide shook his head. "Sorry, probably not on this tour, but we have plenty of shipwrecks around these islands. We never know exactly what lies on the ocean floor because the water currents move

"Pirates! Come quick!" Riley yelled from the hotel balcony.

Uncle Max laughed, and patted Riley on the back. "Carrot Top, you are right. That is the Jolly Roger, a ship created to give tourists a glimpse of pirate life. How would you like to be a pirate for a morning?"

"Really?" Riley could not wait!

"Ahoy, matey!" said a swashbuckling pirate.

Riley stared in amazement as pirates jumped down from the rigging and dueled with swords.

Later that day a boat took them to a nearby reef. "Enjoy your chance to snorkel! Do not touch the coral, watch out for moray eels, and let me know if you find any treasure," laughed the captain.

"Treasure?" asked Riley.

"I am kidding about the treasure, but serious about the eels and coral. If you surprise an eel, it could bite you. Coral is alive and an important part of the reef. Touching or stepping on it can damage or even kill it. Without the coral, fish would have no reason to stay, and we would have nothing left to see."

"Our last stop is Stingray City," the captain said. As he slowed down the boat, they could see people standing in shallow water. Swimming among them were dark, mysterious forms. "Watch those stingrays glide!" said Aunt Martha. "Aren't they graceful!"

STINGRAY CITY

Stingrays first started to gather here when several fishermen dropped their scraps at the sandbar.

Stingrays can grow up to 6 ft., or 2 meters in width.

Careful! They use a barbed spine at the base of their tails to protect themselves.

Riley and Alice slept hard after a full day. The next morning they got up early to play on the beach. "Let's build a treasure chest out of sand and fill it with shells and washed-up coral for jewels," Riley suggested.

"Okay," said Alice. "Maybe we will find some real treasure while we are digging!"

They worked hard as the ocean crept closer. SWOOSH! A big wave washed their treasure out to sea. Tired and hot, they floated on the water.

That afternoon, Uncle Max suggested they all go for a drive around the East End of the island. Their first stop was historic Pedro St. James, one of the oldest buildings on Cayman.

The travelers also saw traditional houses, flower-covered cemeteries and clothes drying in the breeze. They stopped near a rocky overlook.

"Riley, you take the lead," Uncle Max said, with a twinkle in his eye. Riley took a few steps, when a huge wave surged through a hole in the rock and drenched him.

"What was that?" Riley gasped.
"Carrot Top, that is just the blow hole's way of saying hello."

Aunt Martha suggested they stop at the Queen Elizabeth II Botanic Park.

After looking at all of the tropical gardens, Riley and Alice pulled Uncle Max down the trail to find the iguana exhibit.

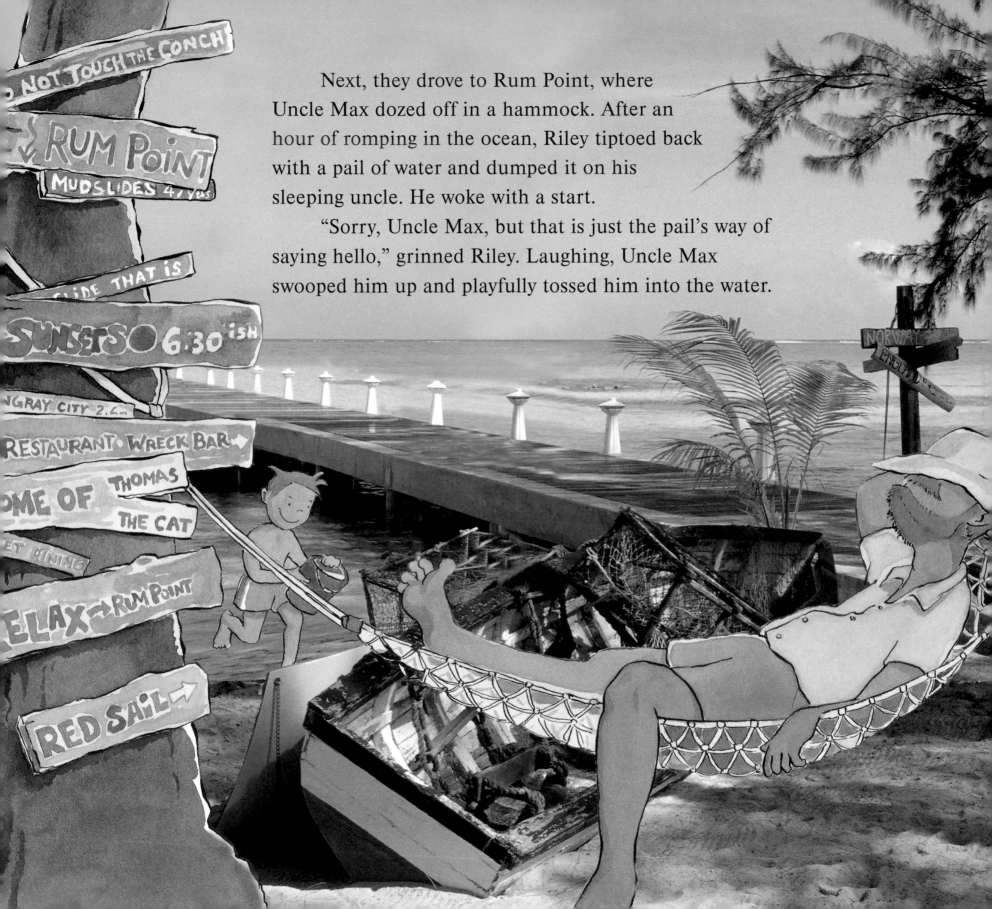

Next, they drove to Rum Point, where Uncle Max dozed off in a hammock. After an hour of romping in the ocean, Riley tiptoed back with a pail of water and dumped it on his sleeping uncle. He woke with a start.

"Sorry, Uncle Max, but that is just the pail's way of saying hello," grinned Riley. Laughing, Uncle Max swooped him up and playfully tossed him into the water.

When they returned to the hotel, Riley and Alice took out their coloring pens and went to work. "What are you two doing?" asked Aunt Martha.

"We are drawing a treasure map," Riley told her solemnly. Alice nodded in agreement.

That night,
they dreamed of
finding treasure.

After breakfast they took a walk on
the beach and rented two jet skis.

"This is so much fun!" yelled Riley, as they bounced over the waves.
Alice nudged her mother. "Look! A turtle!" They slowed down to get a better view.
"What is that?" asked Riley, pointing to a gray box barely visible on the ocean floor.

Uncle Max dove in and came up, out of breath. "It is too heavy to bring up," he panted. "We will have to come back tomorrow when we have more time."

"I knew it. Treasure!" Riley said triumphantly.

Riley and Alice could talk of nothing else but the mysterious box. They finally managed to eat their supper and feed the hungry tarpon fish, which were waiting around the dock for table scraps. Max and Martha watched the sun set in a splendid burst of color.

The whole family played a game of miniature golf to get their minds off the box.

Riley hooted when he saw an enormous pirate's head with its mouth wide open. "There is no escaping the pirates on Cayman. I am going to sink this putt!"

The next day Riley and Alice dragged Uncle Max and Aunt Martha down to the beach. They rented two paddle bikes and took off in search of the treasure box.

When they found it, Uncle Max dove down as everyone held their breath. What would he find?

"That was one tricky box!" Uncle Max spat out as he came to the surface.

"What's in it?" Riley could not contain himself.

Uncle Max looked glum. "I spent ages trying to pry it open, until finally one corner broke off. But when I looked inside, it was nothing but an empty crate."

"Oh," said Aunt Martha. "What a shame. Well, why don't we go buy Riley's mother that rum cake before we have to pack?"

After buying the rum cake, Aunt Martha tried to take a picture of a gloomy Alice and Riley.

Meanwhile, Uncle Max had a little errand to do.

Uncle Max was the last one to pack. He called to Riley and Alice, "I hope you have not packed your swimsuits. We have time for one final visit to the beach, and one last sandcastle."

"I need help with the moat!" Uncle Max called to Riley and Alice, who were splashing in the water. Riley and Alice grabbed their shovels and dug in.

"Look, a Cayman quarter," said Alice, holding a sandy, yellowish coin. Just then Riley's shovel hit something hard. He pulled up another coin.

"Wait a minute, that's no quarter! Let me see your coin." Riley let out a huge yell. "UNCLE MAX! IT'S REAL PIRATE'S GOLD!"

"Aunt Martha, can you believe it? Six real gold coins!" said Riley.

"I bet if we kept shoveling, we could have found an entire pirate's booty," said Alice.

"That is great!" said Aunt Martha, winking at Uncle Max.

He smiled and whispered in her ear, "I only hid four coins." Aunt Martha stared in surprise.

"So we found real treasure in the Cayman Islands," said Uncle Max.

"Yes," agreed Aunt Martha. "Real treasure, in more ways than one."